STAND TALL, MOLLY LOU MELON

To my brother J.Christopher Lovell—Merry Christmas 1976;
and, always, to my mother, Sandra
—P. L.

For Emily Anne, the biggest little girl in the neighborhood
—D. C.

WRITTEN BY **PATTY LOVELL**   ILLUSTRATED BY **DAVID CATROW**

G.P. PUTNAM'S SONS   NEW YORK

G. P. Putnam's Sons,
a division of Penguin Putnam
Books for Young Readers,
345 Hudson Street,
New York, NY 10014.
G. P. Putnam's Sons, Reg. U.S.
Pat. & Tm. Off.
Published simultaneously in Canada.
Manufactured in China by South China
Printing Co. Ltd.
Designed by Gina DiMassi.
Text set in Stempel Schneidler medium.
The art was done in pencil and watercolor.
Library of Congress Cataloging-in-Publication
Data Lovell, Patty, 1964–
Stand tall, Molly Lou Melon / written by Patty
Lovell; illustrated by David Catrow. p. cm.
Summary: Even when the class bully at her
new school makes fun of her, Molly remembers
what her grandmother told her and feels good
about herself. [1. Self-acceptance—Fiction. 2.
Grandmothers—Fiction. 3. Bullies—Fiction.] I.
Catrow, David, ill. II. Title. PZ7.L9575 Mo 2001
[E]—dc21 00-040297
ISBN 978-0-399-23416-3
Special Markets ISBN 978-0-399-25585-4
4 5 6 7 8 9 10

This Imagination Library edition is published by Penguin Young Readers, a division
of Penguin Random House, exclusively for Dolly Parton's Imagination Library,
a not-for-profit program designed to inspire a love of reading and learning, sponsored
in part by The Dollywood Foundation. Penguin's trade editions of this work are
available wherever books are sold.

Molly Lou Melon stood just taller than her
dog and was the shortest girl in the first grade.
She didn't mind. Her grandma had told her,
"Walk as proudly as you can and the world
will look up to you."

So she did.

Molly Lou Melon had buck teeth that stuck
out so far, she could stack pennies on them.
She didn't mind. Her grandma had told
her, "Smile big and the world will smile right
alongside you."

So she did.

Molly Lou Melon had a voice
that sounded like a bullfrog being
squeezed by a boa constrictor.

She didn't mind. Her grandma
had told her, "Sing out clear
and strong and the world will
cry tears of joy."

So she did.

Molly Lou Melon was often fumble fingered.
She didn't mind. Her grandma had told her,
"Believe in yourself and the world will believe
in you too."

So she did.

Then Molly Lou Melon
moved to a new town. She
had to say good-bye to her
grandma and all of her
friends . . .

and start in a new school.

On the first day of school, Ronald Durkin
called her "**SHRIMPO!**" in gym class.

When the game started, Molly Lou Melon
caught the football, ran under the legs of
Ronald Durkin, and scored a touchdown.
All the children thought, "Wow, she's good!"
and Ronald Durkin felt very foolish.

On the second day of school, Ronald Durkin
called her "**BUCKY-TOOTH BEAVER!**"

Molly Lou Melon took out her pennies,
stacked ten high on her teeth, and smiled
as big as day. All the children smiled with glee
and Ronald Durkin felt very foolish.

On the third day of school, Ronald Durkin said, "You sound like a sick duck—**HONK HONK!**"

Molly Lou Melon sang out a "**QUACK!**" so clear and strong that it made Ronald Durkin somersault backwards, hit his head, and have to go to the nurse. All the children cried with joy to be free of Ronald Durkin for the rest of the afternoon and Ronald Durkin felt very foolish.

On the fourth day of school, Ronald Durkin said that she'd made the snowflake all wrong. But Molly Lou Melon opened up her paper and revealed the most beautiful snowflake of all.

All the children oohed and aahed, even Ronald.

On the fifth day of school, Ronald Durkin
brought Molly Lou Melon a stacking penny
for her tooth and smiled at her.

That night Molly Lou Melon took out a pencil
and paper and wrote a letter to her grandma:

Dear Grandma,

I wanted to tell you that everything
you told me was exactly right!

Love,
Molly Lou Melon